Other S

Short Story Collections

Novels

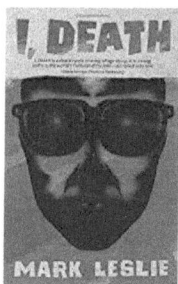

Non-Fiction

ACTIVE READER
AND OTHER CAUTIONARY TALES
FROM THE BOOK WORLD

Mark Leslie

ACTIVE READER

AND OTHER CAUTIONARY TALES
FROM THE BOOK WORLD

Mark Leslie

STARK

PUBLISHING

Active Reader was first published in the February 2008 edition of *Dissections: The Journal of Contemporary Horror*

Browsers was first published in Challenging Destiny #5, January 1999. It was reprinted in *One Hand Screaming* (2004)

Distractions was first published in *World Fantasy Con 2001 CD-ROM* edited by Nancy Kilpatrick. It was reprinted in *One Hand Screaming* (2004)

Stark Publishing
Waterloo, Ontario
www.starkpublishing.ca

The characters and events portrayed in this book are fictitious. Any similarity to real persons, living or dead is merely coincidental and not intended by the author.

Active Reader / Mark Leslie Lefebvre
October 2018

Active Reader is available in print, audio and eBook format

DEDICATION

For Francine and Alexander, my two favorite active readers.

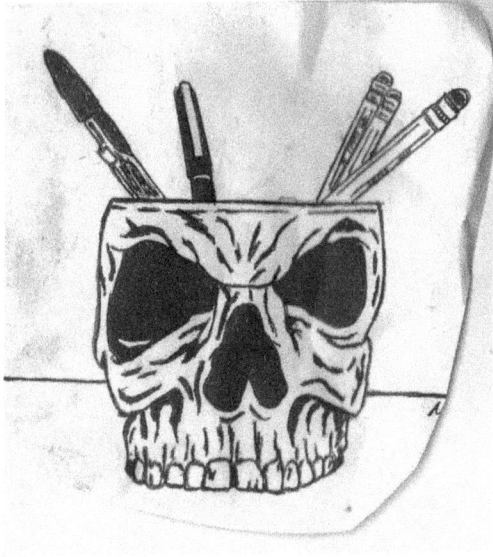

Skull Cup sketch by Mark Leslie

ACTIVE READER

"DO YOU HAVE an Active Reader card?" Douglas smiled across the counter at the pretty young woman as she plopped a pile of paperbacks onto the cash desk.

Her brow creased as she looked at him a moment, then she spied the plastic blue card hanging around his neck on a thin chain – on the card were the words Active Reader, and the NOBLE BOOKS logo of a lion sitting atop a stack of books – and recognition filled her eyes.

"Oh, the discount card. Of course. I always carry it with me." She dug into her wallet and produced the blue NOBLE BOOKS Active Reader card.

Douglas took her card, swiped it through the machine, and then scanned in her books. As he lifted each paperback over the scanner he glanced quickly at the title and author. She has good taste in dark literature, he thought, recognizing some of the titles by Clegg, Campbell, Little and Clarke.

"Oh," Douglas said. *"The Darkest Part of the Woods.* That's a good one. I just finished reading it myself."

She smiled at him. "I love all of Campbell's writing. Both the novels and the short fiction."

"UK's finest horror author."

She nodded enthusiastically.

He pointed at the next book in her pile. "So, have you read other books by this author?"

"Carol Weekes? Oh yes, I've read a couple of hers. She's becoming one of my favorites."

He grinned proudly. "Her writing is a real gift to the horror genre."

The girl nodded, her blonde curly hair bouncing as he continued to scan the books in. Between books, he kept glancing back up at her, noticing the soft blue of her eyes with the subtle green tint. Not only was she very attractive, with sparkling brilliant eyes, but she was also a lover of books and of horror.

That old familiar nervous tingling flitted about his stomach, and he found himself tongue tied, unsure of what to say next. Attractive women didn't do that to him; but an attractive woman with sparkling eyes who loved to read horror sent him into a tailspin.

At the end of the transaction, he announced the total, she paid it and he handed her the books in a NOBLE BOOKS bag and wished her a fond farewell.

As she said goodbye and walked away from the cash desk, Douglas keyed in the code that would reprint the last receipt and then slid the Next Cashier sign onto the desk in front of his register.

"Carrie," Douglas said to the pimply-faced teen working two registers to his left. "I'll be in my office if anyone needs me." With that said he tore off the duplicated receipt and walked away against the background of the Friday night bustling crowd of avid readers, browsers and coffee house regulars.

Closing the door to leave the sounds of the crowd behind him, he glanced down at the receipt.

The top of it read: *Active Reader Member*: 5552 7958.

Douglas fiddled with his NOBLE BOOKS tie and sat down at the computer. He entered the general access password, and then flipped around on the drop-down menu desktop environment until he highlighted the CUSTOMER menu.

He pressed the ENTER key, then typed the management level password which brought him to the customer database. He typed "old" in the command line, and a small window opened, allowing him to enter an eight-digit NOBLE BOOKS Active Reader number.

He entered: 5552 7958.

After a moment, a name, address and phone number appeared on the screen.

"Kim Meadows," Douglas said, reading the customer's name aloud. Then his eyes scanned down to the part of the screen which showed, in detail, all of this particular customer's purchases. The titles, the quantity, the time of day, and how she paid for each purchase. Of course, the database didn't yet include the books she had just purchased. That information was only updated once per day on a national level, once the store closed and the computer uploaded that information to the main database at the NOBLE BOOKS support office.

He scrolled down the huge listing of books she had purchased, at both this location of NOBLE BOOKS and the various locations in other parts of the state, mumbling to himself. "You're quite the active reader, Ms. Meadows." There was a long listing of horror titles, along with thrillers and mysteries. It appeared that Ms. Meadows favored intense, thriller-type reading. It was no wonder she became a fan of Carol Weekes' novels. Carol Weekes was one of a select few authors that Douglas just had to collect every single format in. She was a talented thriller-horror writer who had worked her way up through the small press and onto the tail end of the bestseller lists. Her precise description of details was matched only by her ability to aggressively hammer out characters and a plot that begged you to read for more. From the first time he discovered her first novel Walter's Crossing, Douglas had been a genuine and eager fan, collecting all of her works, no matter if they were small press releases or big publishing house titles.

Finally, after a couple pages of listings he found a few titles by Carol Weekes.

And there, one of the first purchases Kim Meadows had made on her card almost two years ago, at the other NOBLE BOOKS location in the city, was the title he'd been looking for: *It Creeps Up on You.*

"Excellent," Douglas said, smiling and spinning the office chair around. *It Creeps Up on You* was a collection of stories Carol Weekes had published mid-way through her career. It contained a selection of previously un-published works alongside stories that had seen print decades earlier. It was, in Douglas's opinion, the ultimate collection that could be known as the essence of Weekes' writing career, illustrating her as a wicked mystic of the written word. It contained stories filled with hope, horror, laughter, bitter darkness and believable characters. Sure, the title story and some of the others included were stories that Weekes had penned with other authors. But these collaborations only illustrated her unique ability to mesh her own incredible storytelling voice with various other writing talents

Douglas punched the button that would print the screen he was on.

"My collection can now become complete," he said, and a warm fuzzy feeling filled his chest the same way the tingling had filled his stomach when he had been looking Kim Meadows in the eye.

☠ ☠ ☠

Kim Meadows sat curled in a big comfy chair by the window with a down-filled quilt pulled over her. One foot, dressed in a knee-high white sock, dangled out from under the quilt, resting just above where her cat Ginger lay sleeping. On the table beside her sat a steaming mug of lemon tea. Roxy Music's "Avalon" unobtrusively filled the room from the stereo across the room that was dwarfed by huge overflowing bookcases on either side.

She was enraptured in the paperback she had picked up earlier in the week, a thriller by author Michael Slade. She'd never read Slade before, but had caught sight of a display that told her if she liked Tami Hoag, she might also like Michael Slade. She was so enthralled in the novel that she didn't hear the front door to her apartment unlatch itself. Nor did she hear the door slowly open and close.

The only indication that something strange was going on would have been when Ginger sat up for a moment, tilted her head, sniffed the air, then put her head back down on her paws.

With her nose buried in the paperback, and not noticing Ginger, Kim continued to read.

She didn't notice the shadow cast upon the wall to her left, nor did she hear the quiet footsteps approaching her from behind.

She did, however, feel the tip of the blade as it sunk softly into the side of her neck, producing a thin stream of blood.

She turned her head to see a face she recognized but couldn't quite place.

Douglas smiled at her. "I need you to tell me something," he said.

She nodded.

"Have you read everything you bought by Carol Weekes?"

Her eyes widened as she realized where she recognized him from.

"Have you?"

She nodded vigorously.

"Have you read *It Creeps Up on You?*"

She nodded again.

"All of it?"

She grimaced and coughed a small bubble of blood between her lips.

"Did you read all of it?"

She nodded, and he pulled the blade across her throat.

She gurgled something unintelligible and dropped the paperback onto her lap.

A fresh stream of crimson flowed down her chest and onto the paperback as Douglas felt himself harden in anticipation. He sighed. He hadn't read a Michael Slade novel yet. Too bad, he thought vaguely. This particular one had been ruined. But it looked intriguing. Perhaps the next day he would seek out a clean, unbloodied copy off of the store shelves and give it a read.

He sighed aloud and then proceeded to get what he had come for.

Ginger let out a soft mewling and sauntered off to the bedroom.

☠   ☠   ☠

Returning to his home, Douglas poured himself a tall glass of scotch with slivers of thin ice and proceeded to head upstairs into his den. It was time to add his latest addition to the collection.

He stood in the entranceway to the den, flicked on a switch and admired how the tiny display lights he'd installed cast a soft glow onto the covers of his eclectic first edition anthology collection. Even more exciting was the small glass display case filled with formaldehyde resting in front of each book. Several of the display cases – the ones in front of *Tales of Mystery and Imagination* by Edgar Alan Poe, *Alone with the Horrors* by Ramsey Campbell, *A Good, Secret Place* by Richard Laymon, *Death Drives A Semi* by Edo van Belkom and *The Lottery* by Shirley Jackson – had something floating in them already, but the one in front of Carol Weekes' *It Creeps Up on You* was empty.

Douglas stepped forward, reached into his pocket, and pulled out the plastic baggie containing Kim Meadows' eyeballs.

Gingerly, he lifted them out of the baggie and placed them in the formaldehyde of the glass case in front of the book.

Then he smiled a vacant smile as he stood there and sighed, thinking about the years of effort and patience that had brought this collection together. As the memories ran through his head, he inadvertently felt himself hardening again. The excitement began to dwindle as he realized that, with his collection complete, he was again at another crossroads.

What would he collect next?

This is not the time to think about that, he told himself, and went back to admiring his collection in a twisted devotion.

After a few minutes of appreciating the completeness that his new addition added to the collection and sipping at his scotch, he flicked the lights off and left the room. From the den, he wandered over to the guest bedroom and stood there in the doorway. From the darkness within he could make out the shape of his mother who lay in the bed.

As he stood looking at her he could almost hear the quiet snore-like breaths she used to make when she was alive and sleeping. The dimness of the room prevented him from being able to see her waxy-plastic like skin and the fact that her chest was not rising and falling with breath. Taxidermy was a wonderfully useful craft, but the human skin just didn't hold up the way animal pelts did.

His eyes began to mist over, thinking about the tragedy that had befallen the woman her entire life and how she fought back so valiantly, constantly challenging destiny. It was such a shame she had lost her sight when Douglas had been so young. Since he was a child and could put together the words "See Jack Run" she had asked that he read to her. He had quickly become an avid reader, reading her anything from the daily paper to the pocket books he could pick up at the corner store for a mere dime. Even though the traditional roles had been reversed, reading to his mother had been one of the few pleasures Douglas had known.

So when she'd died, almost five years ago, he couldn't do without reading to her.

And as he'd grown his taste in fiction had taken a darker turn.

Perhaps it was reading such things that gave him the idea, but he found that performing some tasks taken from books on taxidermy meant that he could keep his mother with him longer, and share with her even more of the books he loved to read.

The thought of it all made him long for the comfort he'd felt when he recalled one of his very first memories. He was a child, very young and had been troubled in the night. His mother, still able to see – this memory took place before she lost her vision – crawled into bed with him with a storybook and read to him until he relaxed and fell asleep again.

He was tired and hadn't planned on doing any reading tonight, but the feeling of insecurity, wondering what he would do now that his collection was complete, was just too strong. Decisively, he turned, and went back to his den to retrieve the newly acquired eyeballs and the Weekes collection.

Then he returned to his mother's bedroom and flicked on the light to reveal the dead body of a woman who, except for the waxen facial features and the vacant eye sockets, appeared to be sleeping. He gently inserted Kim's eyeballs into the empty eye sockets of his mother's face, slipped beneath the covers to cuddle up beside her, and thumbed the book open to its first page.

"It Creeps Up on You," he read to her in a soft, almost motherly voice. "By Carol Weekes."

.

BROWSERS

"The stimulation of seeing so many books so suddenly seemed almost more than was good for the frail little boy."
-George R. Stewart, **Earth Abides**

STEPPING INTO A used book shop is sometimes like stepping into another dimension. Where else but a used book store can one find such an eclectic selection of minds and experiences stored in dusty tomes, just waiting to be browsed through by anyone who happens along?

Occasionally a used book shop can be a painful experience, offering up nothing more than the latest trashy paperbacks and adult porn magazines.

But sometimes . . .

Sometimes a used book store can provide, to the avid browser, a mystical experience. Sometimes, walking through that door, you are overwhelmed with a sense of awe, a sense that something powerful is being housed within the very walls.

I discovered such a wondrous shop years ago on the corner of two streets whose names I cannot remember in one of those pseudo-cities on the south western edge of the Golden Horseshoe.

Standing on the street, the sounds of traffic all around me, I beheld the quaint corner shop with curious eyes. The dark and dusty windows did not allow me a clear view of the interior of the shop, and apart from the word BROWSERS painted on the window there was no exterior sign indicating the name of the establishment.

Trying to remember if I'd been to this particular shop before, I opened the door. The tiny bell overhead tinkled as I stepped inside. I had to pause as the familiar feeling of awe overtook me. Perhaps you feel it, too, when you walk into a used book shop – the feeling that all eternity is poised, trapped in the moment, just waiting to spill forth into the future.

Literature has always fascinated me. With writing, humankind has developed the ability to elevate a person to a state of immortality. And with that, anyone who reads can thus share in that immortal bliss. None of us have ever had the pleasure of meeting Shakespeare or Dickens personally, but they are still companions in our day to day travels. Though long dead, they are very much with us. That is the beauty and power of literature.

Perhaps that is why I had spent the last three decades of my life writing, trying to capture the spirit of myself on paper. To that point, I had been unsuccessful, forced to live vicariously through the bold efforts of those great masters who'd come before me.

That is probably why I would take such pleasure in browsing through a used book shop. And occasionally, when feeling daring, I would fantasize about future generations browsing such a shop and finding one of my works – essentially discovering my spirit and thus keeping me alive.

The absence of a book clerk was the first thing I noticed. But that wasn't unusual. He or she could be shelving books or helping another customer. Standing in the tiny entranceway I glanced at the small podium desk, which I assumed the owner used as a work space. My eyes then led forward to the next connected room which was perhaps eight by twelve feet. I moved into it. This room, crammed with the usual variety of books, led off directly to another room of similar size.

Trying to get my bearings, I searched through the second room to find two more doorways to a third and forth room. I took the door on the right and found, from that room, another three choices.

The peculiarity struck me at that point. I paused and breathed in my amazement. What looked like such a tiny corner shop was actually a huge space divided into a multitude of rooms.

I saw myself spending a lot of time here.

I decided to waste no more time and began my browsing. I turned and scanned the books that filled the room I stood in. The shelves reached all the way up to the nine-foot ceiling of the room and were packed, tightly, with all sorts of books. Scanning the titles, I noticed that there was no particular order to them. There was an abundance of westerns and the occasional thriller shelved in this room; but apart from that, there was a plethora of every other imaginable type of book. From a selection of children's picture books to a sampling of cheap dime paperbacks, this room had it all. On the far wall sat a selection of magazines and comic books. Beside that were stacks of yellowed newspapers.

"What an interesting setup," I muttered, and my voice carried strangely through the room. My words broke a silence so thick, I might have been standing in an ancient Egyptian tomb. I turned, as if trying to catch my words and take them back so that I might not wake the sleeping texts. But alas, my words were out and lost to me forever.

As I turned I looked through the entrance to another room I hadn't seen before, and a paperback book spine leapt out at me as if highlighted. I stepped into that room and plucked the book from the shelf. It was one of my favourites from a long time back. George R. Stewart's *Earth Abides*. I held it in my hand like a trophy.

I thumbed it open and sniffed at the wonderfully musty smell that can hardly be described so much as it is loved by a bibliophile. Then I flipped through to the middle of the book and began reading, but not aloud. I dared not speak anything else aloud for fear of ruining, again, that special silence.

I read a passage that had stuck with me all these years. The main character, Ish, upon rebuilding a small civilization after the world had been ravaged by plague, takes the boy Joey to one of the libraries left over from before Year One.

Halfway through this scene I noticed that certain words from this passage were missing, as if the ink from the page had dissolved. I flipped through to another passage. Sure enough, the same thing seemed to have happened there as well.

I put the book down and picked up another one. Again, several passages throughout that text were blank – in some places complete lines were missing. I tried another to find the same results, randomly scattered throughout.

I paused and sniffed the air, as if I would be able to tell if there were some corrosive elements lurking in the room, slowly removing the ink from the pages. But I could detect nothing.

Instead, I left the books there and moved on into the next room to my right. I selected another paperback and noticed that none of the words were missing from it. I replaced it and moved across the room, grabbing at what appeared to be an old SOCIOLOGY text. Strangely, whole pages and entire chapters were blank.

I had heard stories and read articles stating that the paper itself of some of the oldest books printed were apparently reacting with the air, causing them to disintegrate. I wondered if perhaps a similar thing was happening, here, but to the ink rather than the paper.

Such a thought sent shivers through my being. The books in these rooms were not ancient by any means, and already the words were dissolving to nothing. A discovery like this might seem happenstance to the average person, or perhaps boring to one whose only source of information is the Internet; but to a book lover like myself, it was as if God had stepped down from heaven and announced that the world would soon be ending.

I spent the next ten minutes or so rushing from room to room, picking up different types of books and thumbing through them, trying to discover some sort of pattern. But the dissolution of the words seemed completely random. It wasn't specific to any one room, or any one kind of book – the phenomenon appeared without any detectable pattern.

It then came upon me to try to find the book clerk and point my discovery out to him or her. Or perhaps the book clerk would already have known about this strange occurrence. Perhaps they would explain it to me as a result of the nearby industrial smelters filling the local atmosphere with a highly selective airborne corrosive material.

Only, by that point, I could not quite remember the way I had come. I began a path from room to room, hoping I'd recall having been in one of them. But in the same way that I was unable to detect a pattern in the phenomenon of the dissolving words, I was also unable to recognize any of the rooms I'd passed through.

I called out, once, only to hear my voice echo through the room I was in and bounce out in the many available directions. But, as before when I spoke, I had the strange sensation that my voice would wake the sleeping tomes.

Beginning to panic, I ran. From room to room I ran, first taking every exit to my immediate right, and, when that didn't help, every doorway to my left.

Finally, I collapsed to the floor, out of breath and out of the energy to be panicked any longer. It looks like I might be trapped here for a long time, I told myself. I might as well take my time and map out my movement in the maze of books and rooms – perhaps that would help me.

I pulled a hardback text from the wall and flipped through it until I found a blank page. Digging into the breast pocket of my jacket, I plucked out my Mont Blanc pen – the one I always carried with me. Perhaps it was in case I was overcome with that once-in-a-lifetime inspiration that all aspiring writers dream will come. Perhaps it was a ritual of connecting myself with a writing instrument so that we were mates on the voyage of life. Whatever it was, I was glad to have made the effort, my whole adult life, to carry this pen with me. For that day, it just might be the thing that helped me get out of this unusual dilemma.

I began to scribble down the shape of the room that I was standing in, leaving spaces to the front of myself, to my left and directly behind me where the other rooms joined it. Then, my sketch of that room complete, I entered the room directly in front of me.

A hollow groan boomed through the infinite silence.

The groan steadily became a wail as I paused in the doorway, dropping both pen and book to clamp my hands to my ears. It echoed through my head despite my efforts to keep it out and seemed to swirl around the room, announcing its misery in no uncertain terms.

Then, as suddenly as it had begun, it stopped.

I turned on the spot, almost afraid to see what had caused that horrid sound. But there was nothing in the room behind me. Nothing, of course, but the books and the shelves that had always been there.

There was no way I was going to go back into that room. Whatever caused that sound might be lurking around the corner. I considered my pen and the book I'd dropped just inside the room and decided to abandon my plans of mapping out the place.

I then wandered, almost casually considering how startled I'd been, from room to room. Occasionally, I would stop to examine a book which caught my eye. I did this – according to my wristwatch – for about three hours.

During this time, I discovered a couple more abnormalities. The first notable one was that a good deal of the books I examined lacked a copyright page. I wasn't sure whether to chalk it up to the same phenomenon that caused the ink to disappear or if it was for some other reason.

The second was the physical layout of the rooms. I mentioned earlier that the shelves reached right up to the ceiling, but I believe I failed to note the differing heights of each room. Each room conformed to a slightly different shape and height, almost the way each snowflake is not exactly the same as the next, no matter how similar they at first appear.

It was towards the end of this casual wandering when I was struck with a strange notion. I thought about all the books I'd seen that day which I would love to have purchased. The only problem was that I couldn't find the cashier. How ironic to have such a wonderful choice of books and be unable to purchase any. Not only that, but for the most part to discover, upon beginning to take the time to read the book, that it was not actually complete -- that it was missing words, lines, complete pages.

I wondered, for a moment, if I had died and was somehow in a kind of hell for book browsers. The ones who waltz into a store, browse for hours, even sit and read entire chapters and then leave, never once making a single purchase. I laughed at the irony of such a hell and then decided against it. Having worked at a bookstore for my first four years after graduating from college, I knew that if this were such a hell, not only would I not be alone here, but there would barely be room for us all, no matter how endless these rooms seemed.

Still, it was an interesting premise to toss about in my mind while tried to find my way out. Several such notions gnawed at me in the hours I wandered, before I was finally overcome with fatigue and had to sit.

Not long after propping myself up against a bookshelf I must have fallen asleep.

☠   ☠   ☠

I'm not sure how long after that I awoke – but when I did, it felt like no other waking I'd ever experienced. I could still sense the world around me, but I wasn't quite myself anymore.

As best I can describe, I was nothing more than a room stacked with shelf upon shelf of all the books I had read in my life. I was added onto the maze of rooms in this "book shop" and must have somehow been fused into it while I slept.

I can't really say how this happened or who caused it. Perhaps this is part of a natural evolution, which might have started with a single book that gained consciousness; and with human-like consciousness came the fear of disintegration and the desire to multiple and grow.

At least now I understand a little of the weird phenomenon which I had discovered, for it occurs in the books which I house inside of me – inside of the special room which is me.

I hold inside of me all of the texts which I have read over the course of my life. And within those texts are certain words, passages and entire pages which I either skipped over, or which I accidentally missed while reading them. So it wasn't due to some strange chemical in the air, but rather from a reading habit which can occur in even the most fastidious reader.

My consciousness is mostly taken up by the books within my spirit. And being stuck only with them, I am sad that I had not read them more carefully while I'd had the chance. For I have perused them again, countless times. And yes, I am disappointed for having accidentally or intentionally skipped certain parts, for I never will know the words I had missed out on.

As time passes, though, and I'm not sure how much has, I am slowly learning how to extend my consciousness out into the neighboring rooms and peruse any of the same texts my silent companions have read that I might house, hoping to fill in the gaps of my own books. It takes what seems like eternity and quite a bit of concentrated effort, but it can be done. After all, it's not like I don't have the time. But I am leery of a time when that too will not be enough.

What we need is more. We need more things to read and share with each other. And we wait for that day when one will join us who has read all the same books we have but who has also read all the words so we might be enlightened completely.

We have nothing but time, so we wait.

Oh, but soft, I think I hear the entrance bell tinkling. Could it be? Yes, I think it is.

After all this time of browsing through countless bookstores, you have found your rightful resting place. Nice of you to come. Browse to your heart's content. We've been waiting a long time for you to join us.

DISTRACTIONS

MAXWELL WASN'T SURPRISED when the rubber ball smashed through the window and rolled to a stop near his feet. In fact, he hardly flinched as the shards of glass flew through the air, some of them nesting in his blond curly locks.

He'd known it was only a matter of time before the ball being bounced against the side of the house strayed just enough to hit the window.

Maxwell looked down at the signed copy of Andy Robinson's latest self-help bestseller: MAXIM POWER II: GETTING THROUGH DISTRACTIONS. Andy's proud, smiling face (with his unique trademark oversized cleft chin and dimples) on the cover brought the book's first words to his mind.

Distractions should be seen as evil.

Calmly, Maxwell picked up the ball and walked out of the study. The ball was made of Indian rubber, warm and hard with just a little give as he pressed his thumb into it. Tossing the ball into the air and catching it with the same hand, he headed down the hall on his way to the door.

The packed book shelf at the end of the hall caught his eye, as it often did. He paused to run the tips of his fingers across the spines of the books. His fingers stopped on a book with golden lettering down the spine reading: THE BRAZEN HERALD.

He pulled the book off the shelf, admiring the cover lettering, the artwork, the dark winged-dragon silhouette against a purple-red sky, and below that, a blue-black sea, and the lone figure standing in the foreground on the edge of the cliff, mostly in silhouette, the blue and yellow tunic showing, the glinting shine of the sword in hand. Turning the hardcover book in his hand, he admired the black and white photo on the back, how the smiling face captured there resembled him, yet was different. A fuller head of hair, the confident smile of an author still producing. Then he read the text. 'Maxwell Bronte lives with his wife Doris in Arizona and is hard at work on his next novel, furthering the chronicles of Sebastian Eldritch.' He smiled and fondly remembered those days. The novel had been praised and cheered – he had been the talk of the town, described as that *up and coming fantasy writer from the Southwest*, the way that King was the horror writer from New England. He'd been interviewed and featured in all the major Science Fiction & Fantasy journals.

That, of course, had been five years ago. He still hadn't finished the follow up novel about Sebastian Eldritch, the one he had been planning on calling HERALD IN PERIL. No, between that first blockbuster novel and now, he'd gone through two job changes, the loss of his father, a near divorce and a house fire. Getting back to working on his novel had not been a priority during those changes.

The world around you shouldn't decide your priorities for you. Only you can do that.

Until he discovered Andy Robinson, that was, and learned that all of it, all that change, turmoil and upset, was really nothing more than distractions that had been getting in the way of fulfilling his destiny.

He'd bumped into Andy at Roc*Kon, a science fiction convention in Little Rock, just a few months ago. Maxwell was still touring the conventions, riding on his one past publishing success and hoping to revitalize his career by being around other successful authors. He'd ended up reminding himself of a certain television star from 20 years ago whose soul quest seemed to be to work non-stop at rallying fans to help bring back STARSHIP ACADEMY, despite the fact that most of the other main cast members from that series had either all but disappeared from acting or had died.

Minutes after making that realization and wondering if he would be doing this for another fifteen years, he'd gotten off the elevator at the wrong floor, where he'd stumbled into a business leaders' convention, and Andy Robinson, the convention's main speaker. Across from the elevators and just outside the lecture room, Andy was involved in an animated discussion with a few men in suits.

The way he moved, gestured, the passion and excitement in his voice, caught Maxwell's attention immediately. Andy actually reminded Maxwell of a character in his novel, the one faithful companion of Sebastian Eldritch, Marvis Cranley, who was a sometimes sidekick, sometimes court jester, and full-time spiritual advisor. He started watching Andy because of this fascinating parallel, but then continued watching him because he was such a captivating speaker. When Andy and the two men (who were also listening to him with rapt attention) moved down the hall, Maxwell spotted the poster-board bearing Andy's grin, and a table covered with the man's motivational books.

The phone began to ring, bringing him out of his silent reminiscence. Maxwell turned and regarded the phone, answering machine and key cup on the small table near the front door.

You can only deal with one distraction at a time. Don't let them gang up on you.

He slid the novel back into place on the shelf between THE ARMIES OF DAYLIGHT by Barbara Hambly and FROSTWING by Richard A. Knaak, two of his favorite fantasy authors. The answering machine picked up after the second ring.

"Hi, Sweetie." His mother's voice, slightly tinny coming through the answer machine speaker, filled the hallway. "I'm just worried because I haven't heard from you in a couple of days. Call me." Damn woman, he thought, continuing his journey down the hallway, making him call her twice a week, as if there were anything important to discuss that often. What a waste of time.

Without breaking stride, Maxwell ripped the phone cord out of the wall and carried the unit out the door. In the entranceway, he lifted the lid off the trash can and dropped the phone inside. "I'm busy, Mom," he said as he snuggled the lid back into place. "I'll deal with you later."

Put aside those extra distractions until you have the time to deal with them.

Maxwell then rounded the house. In the front yard, a red-haired kid with a speckling of freckles across his nose stood waving his arms in the air. It was his neighbor's kid, Danny.

"Sorry, Mr. Bronte. I'm so sorry."

Reaching the boy, Maxwell stopped. "Danny, what did I say about throwing the ball against the side of my house?"

Danny didn't answer.

"Danny. What did I say?"

The boy shifted his left foot in front of his right one, softly digging his toe into the grass as he looked up. "You said not to."

"Not to what?"

"Not to throw the ball against the house because it distracts you when you're –"

"That's right," Maxwell said, cutting the child off. "And you disobeyed me. *Again.*"

"I'm sorry, Mr. Bronte. I'm sorry. Can I have my ball back?"

As Maxwell stood there looking at the boy, he was re-minded of the fact that this distraction was taking up even more of his time. Andy Robinson's smooth calm voice of reason filled his head. *Distractions are anti-trac-tion. You must give yourself traction by eliminating dis-traction.*

"Eliminate distraction," Maxwell mumbled. "You want your ball? Here!" He drew his arm back, and with that, the boy immediately stopped sobbing. He started to stumble backwards, his wide eyes never leaving the ball, as Maxwell followed through on his pitch and sent the ball straight at the boy's head.

The ball bounced off the boy's forehead, the shock, more than anything, dropping him to the ground on his backside.

"And stay out of my yard!"

The boy turned, scrambled forward about a foot on his hands and knees, then got to his feet and ran across the yard to the neighbor's house.

After watching the boy run inside and hearing the sat-isfying slam of the door, Maxwell stood there a moment, taking in a breath of fresh air, carried in on a dry warm desert wind. Then he headed back into the house.

"Oh great," he said, noticing the grass stains on his hand that must have come from the ball. "Running out of time, here."

Andy's voice came to him again. *Time is your friend, not your enemy. Embrace it. Make the most of it.*

He glanced at his watch as he headed toward the bath-room. He only got one day off a week to work on his writing and so far he'd been wasting it with minor distractions. But, as he now knew, *there is no such thing as a minor distraction. Every single distraction is evil and must be dealt with or they will soon stockpile and run your life.* For the past five years, he'd let distractions get in his way. They'd stockpiled in front of him, preventing him from getting anything accomplished. Job Interviews, Funerals, Marriage Counsellors. Distractions with capital letters, all of them, preventing him from getting down to his novel. But not anymore.

Not with the sound words of Andy Robinson to inspire him along.

When Maxwell got to the washroom, he turned on the water, not bothering to wait for the hot water to start coming out. No. That would be a waste of time. He smiled at himself in the mirror as he washed his hands. The new Maxwell smiled back at him.

Say goodbye to the you that says, 'Perhaps I'll do it later.' And say hello to the you that says, 'I want it right now!'

The new Maxwell didn't procrastinate and thought of time as his best friend. *Because time was too powerful to work against.*

Hey, that was a good one he'd just made up on his own.

Not only was Maxwell taking charge of his life, but he was able to rework Andy's strong and powerful words into his own life. After all, it was Andy who said: *Don't just follow these tips blindly. Take them. Use them as your own, and they will evolve into your own words, your own tips, your own maxims.*

Still smiling, Maxwell felt something soft and furry rubbing up against his leg. He looked down at an orange tabby, Smuckers, as it purred and wound back and forth between his legs. Maxwell's smile began to falter as it continued this pattern without pause. And he knew it wouldn't stop until the animal was either fed or petted or perhaps both.

In any case, it was just another distraction.

Still smiling, Maxwell scooped the tabby up, carried it to the toilet and forced its head under the water. Within a couple of minutes, the struggling was over, and he set the toilet lid back down, the cat's orange tail still sticking out. He'd been surprised that the feline hadn't put up more of a fight.

Soon, he would have to clean the body out of there. But he couldn't worry about that now. He had to remain focused on the job at hand.

Prioritize your list. What is important? What can wait?

As he washed his hands, Maxwell became aware of a stinging sensation on his left arm. He turned his wrist over and discovered that the cat must have indeed fought back at least a little. There, on his skin, was a puffed-up red scratch. The center of the scratch had opened and a thin line of blood leaked out.

"Not another distraction," Maxwell mumbled, opening up the medicine cabinet. Unable to find any bandages, he stormed out into the hallway.

The doorbell rang.

Maxwell turned towards the door.

On the other side of the screen door stood his neighbor, Gus Sherrington. Gus looked like a much older version of his son, Danny, complete with the thick patch of freckles across his nose. But his red hair had receded to nothing more than a patch of wispy tufts a few inches above each ear. The way he was breathing, in big dramatic gasps, and the look on the man's face suggested that Gus was none too happy that Maxwell had beaned his son with the Indian rubber ball.

Gus raised a baseball bat where Maxwell could see it. "Get yoh ass out heah!" he screamed through the door. "I'll kick yoh ass down the frickin' street for touchin' mah boy."

Distractions have a way of compounding themselves, becoming more than the sum of their parts. "No kidding," Maxwell mumbled, stepping over to the closet. He opened the closet door and reached in for his shotgun.

Eliminating distractions, at any cost, is often your only solution.

"Get yoh ass out heah!" Gus yelled again, unable to see Maxwell checking to ensure the gun was loaded behind the cover of the closet door.

"Ah said . . ." Gus started to say, but stopped as Maxwell closed the closet door and revealed the gun. Gus's eyes were suddenly as wide as his son's had been when he knew he was going to be getting his ball back the fast and hard way.

Stepping forward and raising the shotgun to chest level, Maxwell fired. The glass and screen shattered in an explosive blast, and Gus was knocked backward off his feet, almost as much from the sound as from the force hitting him in the chest.

Maxwell stepped forward, looking at the man lying on the sidewalk on his back. His eyes wide and terrified, were fixed on Maxwell; his chest, now hitching even more dramatically than before, was pretty much a stewed up mess of blood, skin, pellets and the remains of his yellow t-shirt. His right hand still clutched the baseball bat and his left hand pawed at the grass, as if it alone could drag him away from further pain.

Distractions are often over before you stop being distracted by them. Could that be the case now? Certainly, Gus wasn't a distraction any longer; he should let him be.

Maxwell turned and headed back down the hallway.

A trickle of blood leaked down his forehead. He figured it must be a cut from the glass, either from the screen door just now or the glass that flew through the air when the ball came through his window.

Whatever it had been, it signalled a need for more bandages.

He stormed towards the master bedroom. "Doris, where are the bandage–"

He paused at the bedroom door. His wife was lying on the floor, her dead hand still clutching the vacuum cleaner wand.

"Oh yeah," Maxwell muttered, remembering. His wife had had the nerve to start vacuuming when she knew he had a lot of work to get done. What a stupid thing to do. He was going to miss her. Strange how quickly he'd forgotten about killing her.

Once you eliminate a distraction, you should forget that it ever existed. Or else it will consume your mind, and your time. That is why distractions are so evil. That is why they must be vanquished.

He decided enough time had been wasted. Without Doris around to help find the bandages, he'd probably never locate them.

Instead, he headed back to his den. He sat in front of the computer, smiled as he propped the shotgun against his desk and lifted his coffee, now cool, to his lips, and relished in the silence of the afternoon.

Now that the distractions were removed, he could get some work done.

After all, there was only so much time to write.

Off in the distance, a wailing siren started to lurk up out of the silence.

Unless it pertains to you directly, ignore anything that threatens to distract you. Deal with it only when it begins to directly interfere with your goal.

Maxwell sent a sideways glance at the shotgun propped up against his desk and then typed, figuring he could at least finish his next paragraph before the police car reached his house.

As he typed, Andy Robinson's smiling face watched him proudly from the cover of the book.

ACTIVE WRITER

Notes from the Author

THIS SECTION IS a quick look at the writing of the three tales appearing in this particular chapbook. If you are a person who enjoys a "behind the scenes" look at the creation of a story, or are interested in what originally inspired an author to write a tale, then you might enjoy what is to come.

If, however, you don't enjoy such tangents to the enjoyment of reading fiction, then I advise you to stop here. The fiction, the suspension of disbelief aspect is now complete. Nothing more for you to see here. Thanks for checking it out.

But if you do enjoy such diversions, time's a wastin' – flip that page and continue to enjoy the read.

A Note on This Chapbook

All of these stories have previously been published. This chapbook was an attempt to draw together three decidedly different tales I wrote drawn from the darker or twisted side of the book world.

The original version of this chapbook was put together as an attempt to test out the Espresso Book Machine which arrived at *Titles Bookstore* at McMaster University in the fall of 2008.

Rather than use works from the public domain or attempt to sign legal documents, etc. I figured creating a small book containing works to which I own the rights was a simple and efficient way of getting to that end.

And, of course, anyone who knows me understands that I am a strong advocate of self-promotion for authors -- so if the creation of this book serves to promote my writing, then I'll just have to live with that.

In the spring of 2010, after seeing an incredible demonstration by Smashwords founder Mark Coker at the BookNet Canada Tech Forum in Toronto I wanted to further experiment with digital distribution of my work. Why not, then, put this together in digital format.

If, by reading this digital chapbook in whatever version you chose to consume it, you find yourself enjoying my writing, perhaps you'll check out my full story collection *ONE HAND SCREAMING* (which is still available in print format but also in digital format), or one of my many other digital story collections at a variety of other places where digital books are available.

Active Reader

First appeared online in the February 2008 edition of Dissections: The Journal of Contemporary Horror

This story is one that sat in the back my head for a long time before I sat down to write it. The concept was born out of a desire to write a procedural crime investigation story.

Let me step back and explain.

When I sat down to write this tale, I was still working for Canada's largest book retailer, which had an incredible discount card/loyalty program. One of the benefits of such a program involves a business process known as CRM (Customer Relationship Management). Loyalty, memberships and discounts cards (and not just the ones available in bookstores) are used not just to entice customers to get discounts or build up reward points -- they are used strategically to save marketing dollars.

In a nutshell, understanding which of your customers purchase which types of products allow you to send specific messages and promotions to ONLY those individuals who are more likely to take advantage of them. IE, in the case of a bookstore, if they want to market a new mystery book, they can either spend their money advertising the book's availability or special discount this week/month to the general public and perhaps get the attention and sales they desire. Or, if they send that message to a targeted market of individuals who have a history of purchasing mystery novels, then they are more likely to realize a greater return on that investment of resources.

From the customer viewpoint, it also makes sense. As a reader of mystery novels, I'm not particularly interested for my favourite bookstore to send me messages about what new philosophy book is now out -- but if they send me information on the latest mysteries by Canadian authors, then I'm more likely to pay attention and actually read these messages.

Such details and knowledge about my preferences are easily extracted from my own history as a shopper.

Without getting into a discussion about privacy issues, customer loyalty programs exist in almost every single retail environment. They are usually locked down and can only be accessed by particular individuals within an organization.

However, concepts drawn from the darker shadows of my mind started to speculate about a person with access to such a database of information. What if they were a little twisted?

At first I was considering writing a tale about a serial killer who decides to stalk and kill everyone who has read a particular book. Perhaps a sort of radical religious crusade to eradicate the world of people who, for example, read horror stories. I was toying with the idea of writing a mystery tale involving detectives who track down a string of murders and find that the connection is they all purchased the same book from a particular bookstore. As the investigation unfolds, one of the detectives, an avid reader, finds the only thing all victims had in common was they bought a particular book from a local book store; and that would lead them to the killer.

But that was too straightforward.

When I started imagining a character who would do such a thing, I thought it would be more interesting to view the tale through their point of view. And when I took on that character's point of view, the concept of their specific type of derangement took on a different look and feel.

Douglas, my main character, didn't have a vendetta against people who read a particular book. Instead, he was a collector. A twisted, misguided collector with perhaps a little bit of Norman Bates thrown in.

In terms of a membership program, the existing one at Canada's major chain retailer was called an AVID READER card, which has since evolved into another name. I couldn't realistically use an existing card, but quite liked that name; this is where the term ACTIVE READER came from -- and I was satisfied with that name it because it did a decent job of sounding real and getting across the point. People who buy a lot of books are likely very active readers.

I threw elements from the United States into the story merely for commercial purposes. Let's be honest here -- there are simply more markets available to writers in the US than there are in Canada. So why not set the story there and stand a slightly better chance of appealing to where most of the readership is likely to be from? And thus I wrote in details and descriptions that might remind customers of a large US bookstore chain. Of course, no malice was intended against any particular bookseller -- I was just hoping that the familiarity with existing loyalty programs might add an element of reality to this cautionary tale.

Here are a couple more fun points about this tale which some readers might see as "Easter Eggs."

This story is, in many ways, an ode to a friend of mine who is an extremely talented writer. While the details and "history" of one of the writer's mentioned in this story are fictitious, Carol Weekes is a brilliant writer whom I'm sure is going to see much of the success that I predict for her in this tale. WALTER'S CROSSING was indeed her first novel -- but everything else written about her (except for her brilliance and the fact that she co-wrote a story entitled "It Creeps Up On You") are completely fictitious. Keep your eyes peeled for her writing. In late 2009, Carol and Michael Kelly's novel OUROBOROS came out to some incredible reviews – and for good reason – both Carol and Michael are extremely talented writers. You will definitely not be disappointed should you check out either of these authors.

As a creative exercise, I thought I might also throw in a few references to my own publishing history over the past decade or so. I was able to work the names of several different small press horror magazines in which my writing appeared into this story. If you like looking for "Easter Egg" references in fiction and are familiar with my work, you might have fun looking for them.

Browsers

First published in Challenging Destiny #5, January 1999

I have already written a detailed account of the origin of this story, which appeared in my 2004 collection *ONE HAND SCREAMING* (still available in print and in digital format). I am thus a bit leery of repeating things I have already mentioned; but for those reading "Browsers" for the first time, I'll offer up a "Reader's Di-gest" version of the writing of this tale.

"Browsers" was based on one of my earliest experiences exploring bookstores in downtown Hamilton. The description of the bookstore in this story is derived from an actual shop I got lost in one weekend afternoon while exploring various bookstores in the city.

When "Browsers" was first reprinted in my book *ONE HAND SCREAMING,* I was doing a book signing at the Coles in Limeridge Mall on Hamilton Mountain. One of the people who stopped by to chat with me and purchase a copy of the book was a young man who was a book lover. When we started talking about our love of books and bookstores, he mentioned that he knew every single bookstore in the city. I described my story "Browsers" to him and explained that it was based on a bookstore in Hamilton I'd been to several years earlier, but that I hadn't been able to find it since. He said he would read it with interest and see if he could determine which one it was.

A couple of weeks later when I was doing a book signing at the Chapters in Ancaster, the same young man approached me. He said that when he read "Browsers" he recognized the particular bookstore I had been trying to describe. We exchanged memories of the place and he told me it had gone out of business a few years earlier.

Needless to say, I was a bit relieved to learn that the bookstore did actually exist and that it wasn't some sort of freakish "Twilight-Zone" experience I had imagined.

"Browsers" was first published in the Canadian speculative fiction magazine Challenging Destiny in 1999, and reprinted in my collection in 2004. But in March 2008 a slightly revised version of the story (and the one that appears here) was published in the anthology *BOUND FOR EVIL: Curious Tales of Books Gone Bad* published by Dead Letter Press. This is a beautiful collection of almost 800 pages of stories about books edited by Tom English and limited to 500 copies. A deluxe smythe-sewn hardcover bound in imitation leather stamped in golfleaf, this beautiful book is a treasured favorite of mine.

Speaking of favorites, "Browsers" is one of my favorite stories, not only because it is references bookstores and the love of books, but because I believe it is indicative of the type of "quiet" horror and speculative fiction I enjoy writing.

Distractions

First appeared in World Fantasy Con 2001 CD-ROM edited by Nancy Kilpatrick

Similar to "Browsers," Distractions also appeared in my 2004 collection *ONE HAND SCREAMING*. And I'd hate to repeat what I said about the story there, so I'll do my best not do.

This particular story, which features a frustrated writer, is an example of the type of dark humor that I'm often quite fond of producing in my fiction.

The cautionary element in this tale involves the main character's unwavering belief that he is going to find the answers to all of his woes within the pages of a popular self-help book. Having been a bookseller for over sixteen years, I have seen more than my fair share of self-help books climb to the top of the bestseller lists and the lem-ming-like behavior otherwise intelligent people display in terms of unquestioningly following the advice of self-proclaimed gurus.

I thought it would be fun to examine what might happen if an unsuspecting author, frustrated with trying to squeeze writing time into his life, fell victim to the mantras and overly simplistic belief system that a self-help guru preaches.

Though he is a murderer, Maxwell Bronte is as much a victim in this story as anyone. Though there is no actual sentient nature to Andy Robinson's book in this story, the book itself is meant to be seen as some sort of shadowy evil presence, affecting and controlling Maxwell's weakened mind.

ABOUT THE AUTHOR

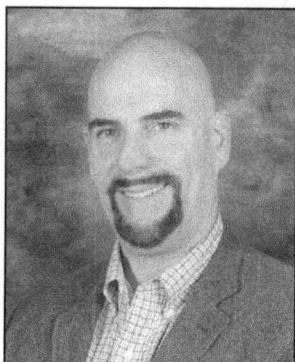

Mark Leslie is a writer, editor and bookseller who was born and grew up in Sudbury, Ontario, spent many years in Ottawa, Ontario and currently lives in Southern Ontario.

A bookselling veteran for more than twenty years, Mark has worked at virtually every type of bookstore, has sat on the Board of Directors for BookNet Canada and also been President of the Canadian Booksellers Association, was the Director of Self-Publishing and Author Relations at Kobo from 2011 to 2017 and is currently Director of Business Development for Draft2Digital. He has given talks across Canada and the United States, in London, Paris and Frankfurt on the bookselling, writing and publishing industry.

You can learn more about Mark and sign up for his newsletter at www.markleslie.ca.

Other Books by Mark Leslie

Canadian Werewolf

This Time Around (Prequel / Short Story)

A Canadian Werewolf in New York

Fear and Longing in Los Angeles (coming soon)

The Desmond Files

Evasion

Coversion (coming soon)

Sin Eater

Collateral Damage (Short Story)

I, Death

Short Story Collections

One Hand Screaming

Active Reader: And Other Cautionary Tales from the Book World

Snowman Shivers

Nocturnal Screams: Night Cries

Short Stories

A Murder of Scarecrows

Spirits

Anthologies (as Editor)

Campus Chills

Tesseracts Sixteen: Parnassus Unbound

Fiction River: Editor's Choice

Fiction River: Feel the Fear

Fiction River: Feel the Love

Fiction River: Superstitious

Non-Fiction / Paranormal / Ghost Stories

Haunted Hamilton

Spooky Sudbury

Tomes of Terror

Creepy Capital

Haunted Hospitals

Macabre Montreal

Watch for more at www.markleslie.ca.

Printed in the USA
CPSIA information can be obtained
at www.ICGtesting.com
JSHW021414060924
69339JS00004B/181